This storybook belongs to:

....

Retold by Mandy Archer

Endpaper illustration by Estelle Corke

A catalogue record for this book is available from the British Library

Published by Ladybird Books Ltd
80 Strand, London, WC2R 0RL
A Penguin Company

001-2 4 6 8 10 9 7 5 3 1
© LADYBIRD BOOKS LTD MMXII
Stories previously published in Ladybird Favourite Fairy Tales for Girls © MMXI

ISBN: 978-0-71819-911-1

Printed in China

Ladybird

TRADITIONAL
TALES
FOR
GIRLS

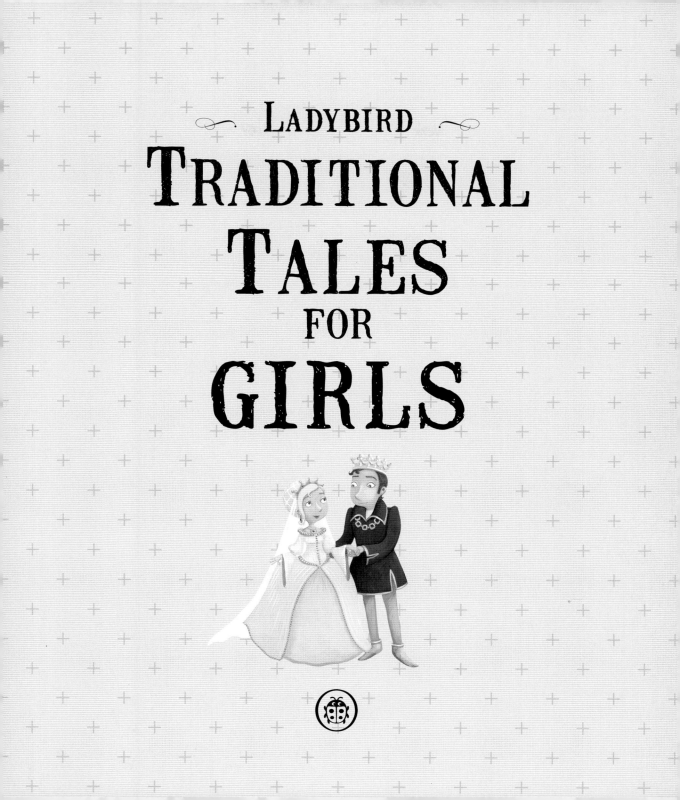

Contents

SLEEPING BEAUTY

CINDERELLA

ONCE UPON A TIME there was a beautiful young girl called Cinderella. She lived in a small cottage with her stepmother and two stepsisters. Even though Cinderella was gentle and kind, the stepsisters and their mother treated her cruelly.

Every morning, Cinderella had to do all the housework.
While she scrubbed, cleaned, tidied and cooked, her
stepmother and stepsisters sat eating cake and drinking tea.

One day, the stepsisters were very excited. The prince of the kingdom had invited them to attend a special ball at the royal palace!

"Am I invited, too?" Cinderella asked in a tiny voice.

The stepsisters both shook their heads.

"How can you come?" screeched the first stepsister. "Your dress is stitched out of rags."

The second stepsister pointed at Cinderella's bare feet. "Look! You don't even have any shoes to wear."

Cinderella stared sadly down at her careworn clothes. She didn't have the lovely gowns her stepsisters did.

The stepsisters left for the ball, admiring each other's fine outfits.
"The prince is sure to want to marry one of us!" they cackled.

Suddenly, a fountain of sparkles shimmered in the doorway. A lady with a friendly smile came into the room.

"Hello, Cinderella," she said. "I am your fairy godmother. You *shall* go to the ball."

The fairy godmother waved her star-topped wand. Cinderella gasped as a stunning pink gown and a pair of glass slippers appeared!

Cinderella quickly got dressed. The pink gown and delicate glass slippers fitted perfectly!

The fairy godmother led the girl out to the front garden. She pointed her magic wand at a pumpkin and then at two mice playing in the grass. In an instant the pumpkin was transformed into a beautiful coach. The mice became majestic white horses.

Cinderella got ready to leave.

"Make sure you're home before the last chime of midnight," warned the fairy godmother. "That's when the spell will break."

When Cinderella arrived at the palace, no one recognized her in such fine clothes. Everyone was talking about the mysterious, beautiful girl in the pink dress.

The prince was enchanted from the very first moment that he saw Cinderella.

"May I have this dance?" he asked, twirling her round and round the ballroom.

It was the most wonderful evening of Cinderella's life. The prince danced only with her until the clock struck twelve. Cinderella gasped when she heard the chimes.

"It's midnight!" she whispered. "I have to leave."

Cinderella left the palace ballroom as fast as she could.

"Come back!" begged the prince. "I don't even know your name."

The poor girl knew she couldn't stop – the magic was going to disappear at any moment!

In her rush to leave, Cinderella lost one of her glass slippers on the staircase.

The prince watched her go, clutching the shoe in his hand.

Cinderella ran home as fast as she could. By the time she crept into bed, her dress had become rags once more.

The prince travelled the kingdom searching for the stranger who had captured his heart.

"I will marry the girl whose foot fits this slipper," he announced.

One day, he and his footman turned into the lane where Cinderella lived.

The stepsisters showed the
prince into their house, desperate
to try on the glass slipper.

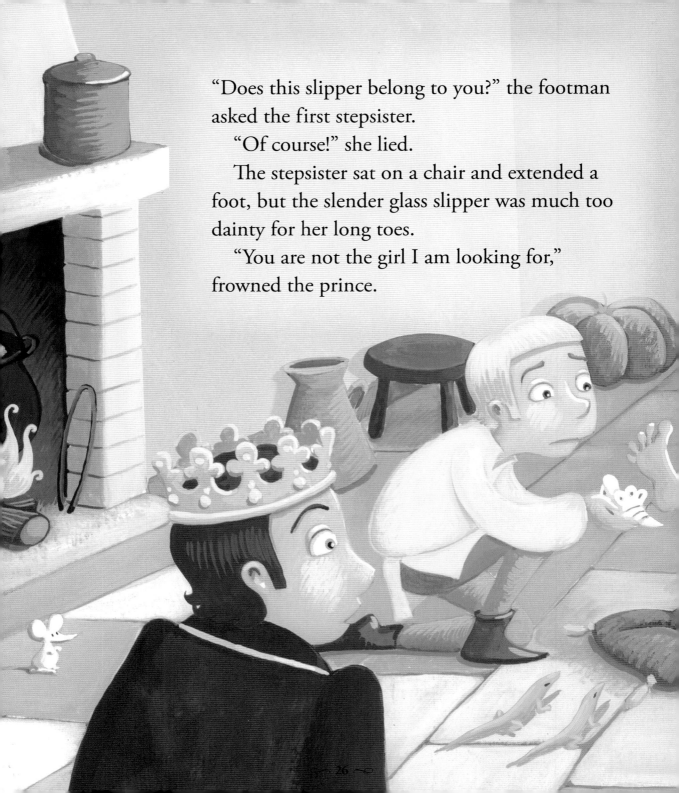

"Does this slipper belong to you?" the footman asked the first stepsister.

"Of course!" she lied.

The stepsister sat on a chair and extended a foot, but the slender glass slipper was much too dainty for her long toes.

"You are not the girl I am looking for," frowned the prince.

Cinderella watched nervously
in the background.

The second stepsister pushed herself in front of the prince.

"It must be me, sire!" she grinned.

She tried and tried to wedge her toes into the shoe, but it was hopeless. The slipper was much too small for her chubby foot.

"Is there anyone else?" asked the prince.

Cinderella blushed, then stepped forwards.

"May I try, Your Majesty?" she asked.

The prince gently slipped the glass slipper on to her elegant foot. It fitted perfectly.

"At last!" he cried. "I have found my beautiful princess."

The prince didn't care about Cinderella's rags. Instead he saw the enchanting girl who had won his heart in the palace ballroom.

"Will you marry me?" he asked.

Cinderella agreed at once. The prince immediately whisked her away to the palace, where they lived happily ever after.

LITTLE RED RIDING HOOD

ONCE UPON A TIME, there was a young girl who lived with her mother and father in a little house at the edge of the forest. She was known as Little Red Riding Hood because she loved to wear a beautiful cloak made out of scarlet velvet.

One morning, Little Red Riding Hood's mother had a special errand for her.

"Your grandmother is ill," she explained. "Please take her this basket of cakes."

"Of course!" smiled Little Red Riding Hood.
She decided to set off straight away.

Little Red Riding Hood's grandmother lived on the far side of the forest. The walk was dark and lonely, but Little Red Riding Hood had made the journey many times before.

"Make sure that you stay on the path," said her father, waving goodbye.

Her mother gave her a kiss. "And say a polite good morning to Grandmother."

"I will," nodded Little Red Riding Hood.

Little Red Riding Hood's mother and father did not know that a wolf lived in the forest. He was a fierce old beast with sharp teeth and cunning yellow eyes. The wolf sniffed the air. He was feeling especially hungry today.

As she walked along the path, Little Red Riding Hood sang a song to herself. She didn't spot the wolf listening from behind a tree, his yellow eyes blazing.

"She'll make a fine supper!" he decided.

The wolf crept out of sight, then dashed through the trees as fast as his legs could carry him. He didn't stop running until he reached the cottage where Little Red Riding Hood's grandmother lived. The wolf knocked gently on the front door.

"Come in," called a weak voice.

The wolf burst into the room. Quick as a flash, he rolled the old woman up in a rug and hid her under the bed. He quickly put on her nightgown and bonnet.

A while later Little Red Riding Hood skipped up the path, eager to see her beloved grandmother. She knocked on the front door.

"Come in!" called a gruff voice.

Little Red Riding Hood's heart fluttered. Her grandmother sounded very strange today!

Little Red Riding Hood stepped nervously into her grandmother's cottage. She could see the old lady sitting up in bed, knitting a pair of socks, but something about her seemed funny.

"Come closer, my dear," said the wolf, trying to make his voice sound reedy and soft.

When Little Red Riding Hood walked up to the bed, the wolf pulled the patchwork quilt up to his chest.

"Oh, Grandmother," said the girl. "What big ears you have!"

The wolf nodded and beckoned for her to come even closer.

"All the better to hear you with, my dear," he replied.

Little Red Riding Hood stepped forward and gazed into the wolf's face. The sly creature pulled the pink bonnet down a little lower.

"Oh, Grandmother," said the girl. "What big eyes you have!"

The wolf couldn't help licking his lips.

"All the better to see you with, my dear," he agreed.

Having Little Red Riding Hood so close made the wolf feel hungrier than ever. He smiled a broad smile, then got ready to pounce.

"Oh, Grandmother," said Little Red Riding Hood. "What big teeth you have!"

The wolf pulled back the covers and sprang out of bed.

"All the better to eat you with, my dear!" he snarled.

"Help!" screamed Little Red Riding Hood, running for the door. Her poor grandmother could only watch and tremble, still trapped under the bed.

The wolf flashed his claws and bared his teeth, almost tearing the girl's velvet cloak.

Little Red Riding Hood's cries
echoed across the forest. Her father
was out chopping wood when he
heard the commotion.

Little Red Riding Hood's father snatched up his heavy axe. He ran all the way to Grandmother's cottage and stormed inside.

The wolf howled when he saw Little Red Riding Hood's father waving the sharp axe! He ran for his life out of the cottage, still dressed in Grandmother's pink nightgown. He was never seen nor heard of again.

HANSEL AND GRETEL

A LONG TIME AGO, two children lived in a forest with their father and stepmother. Hansel and Gretel were both helpful and kind, but times were hard. Their father was a poor woodcutter who struggled to provide for his family. On many nights Hansel and Gretel had to go to bed without any supper.

The family got poorer and poorer until one day the few coins they had ran out.

"We cannot feed four mouths," snapped the stepmother. "The children must go."

The woodcutter begged his wife to change her mind, but she wouldn't give in. Hansel and Gretel listened at the door as their stepmother plotted to abandon them in the forest.

The next morning, Hansel and Gretel's stepmother woke the children early.

"Get up!" she snapped. "We're going to collect wood from the forest."

As their parents marched ahead, Hansel dropped a trail of pebbles along the path. He'd had the good sense to creep out and collect them the night before.

When they reached the darkest part of the forest, Hansel and Gretel's father hugged them tightly.

"Wait here until we've finished chopping wood," he said.

The children waited until it got dark, but their father and stepmother didn't return.

"I'm frightened," wept Gretel.

Hansel pointed to the path and smiled. A line of pebbles shone in the silver moonlight.

Hansel and Gretel followed the trail of pebbles all the way back to their cottage.

"Thank heavens you're alive!" cried their father as he opened the door.

His wife stormed back to bed, her furious face twisted in the candlelight.

"We should have led them deeper into the forest," she whispered. "Next time they must never find their way home."

That night Hansel and Gretel's cruel stepmother locked them in their room so they couldn't pick up any more pebbles. As soon as it was daylight, they were taken back into the forest.

Hansel reached into his pocket and pulled out the crust of bread that he'd been given for breakfast. This time he secretly dropped crumbs along the path instead.

The woodcutter looked sad and tired when it was time to say goodbye.

"What shall we do now?" asked Gretel, watching her parents walk away.

"Look for the trail of breadcrumbs," smiled Hansel.

The little girl looked, but there was nothing there. The birds of the forest had eaten up every crumb.

The children walked helplessly through the trees. Suddenly they found themselves in a grassy clearing. There before them was a magical gingerbread house. The door was made of toffee and lollipop flowers dotted the garden. Hansel and Gretel couldn't resist eating a little. Every mouthful was delicious!

"Come in!" cried a little old lady sitting at the window.

As soon as Hansel and Gretel stepped inside, the old lady slammed the door behind them. She was a wicked witch who liked to eat lost little boys and girls.

"Get in here!" she snapped, bundling Hansel into an iron cage. "You'll make a delicious supper!"

The witch dragged Gretel to the kitchen.

"Open the oven door," she snarled. "You'll bake the bread to go with my feast."

Gretel could see that the old crone wanted to cook her, too.

"The oven isn't big enough," she pretended. "How will the bread tray fit in?"

The evil witch hobbled over and flung open the oven door. Flames curled and spat at the pair.

"Look, foolish girl!" she sneered. "It's even big enough for me to fit inside."

Gretel pretended to look. Then, with a great heave, she pushed the witch inside and shut the door.

Gretel unlocked Hansel's cage as fast as she could.

As her brother climbed out, something gleamed on the shelf beside Gretel. The little girl lifted down a chest filled with gold coins.

"We can buy food at last!" cried Hansel.

It took Hansel and Gretel a long time to make their way home. When they finally found the path back to their cottage, their father held his arms out with joy.

"Your stepmother has gone," he explained. "We'll never be parted again."

So the family lived happily ever after in their quiet cottage, surrounded by love and laughter.

SLEEPING BEAUTY

THERE WAS ONCE a king and a queen who longed for a child. After many years, the queen gave birth to a baby girl. The royal couple were so enchanted with their daughter, they invited all the good fairies in the land to become her godmothers.

On the day of her christening, the fairies gathered in the nursery.

The fairies cast spells over the sleeping
baby. Their wands glittered as they
fluttered beside the cradle.

"She will have great beauty,"
pronounced the first fairy.

"She will be clever and wise,"
said another.

Each of the fairy godmothers had their own
special gift for the new princess.

Just when the king and queen thought that their joy was complete, another fairy appeared at the castle window.

"Why was I not invited here today?" she demanded.

The king and queen gasped. They had forgotten that this fairy still lived in the kingdom!

The forgotten fairy was evil. Her green eyes flashed as she darted towards the cradle.

"I have a spell for the princess, too," she hissed. "In sixteen years she will prick her finger on a spinning wheel and die!"

The bad fairy cackled with laughter, then disappeared out of the window. The little princess began to cry.

"What are we to do?" asked the queen, cradling the baby to her chest.

"We must burn every spinning wheel in the land!" the king ordered.

None of the good fairies possessed magic strong enough to break the curse. There was, however, one glimmer of hope.

"I have yet to give my christening spell," said a fairy with golden wings.

A cascade of stardust burst from her tiny wand.

"The princess will not die," she said. "Instead she will prick her finger and fall asleep for one hundred years."

The fairy revealed that only a kiss of true love would be able to rouse the princess from her slumber.

The years passed. The king and queen's beloved daughter grew up to be just as enchanting as the good fairies had promised she would be.

She spent her days roaming the castle and its grounds, singing to the birds and animals.

Everybody adored the princess's kind heart and sweet ways.

One day, the princess discovered a staircase
that she had never seen before.

"What could be up here?" she wondered.

A forgotten spinning wheel stood in the
chamber at the top. When the princess
reached out to touch it, the needle pricked
her finger. She fell asleep straight away.

At the very same instant that the princess cut her finger, every man, woman and child in the kingdom fell into a deep slumber. Even the animals fell asleep.

The castle slept like that for many years. After a time, thorns and brambles grew all over the stone building, hiding it from view.

The story of the mysterious Sleeping Beauty spread far and wide. Many brave knights tried to ride through the briars that covered the castle, but the thorns were too sharp to hack away.

One hundred years went by.

One day a noble prince passed the princess's tower.

"I shall break the fairy's curse," he promised.

The prince had been dreaming of meeting a beautiful princess for a long time. When he raised his sword, the briars parted before him.

He walked through the deserted courtyard and into the silent castle. All around, servants, jesters and villagers lay where they'd fallen asleep one hundred years earlier.

The brave prince climbed the briars all the way up to the top of the tallest turret. He peered in the window and gasped.

"She is even more beautiful than I imagined," he whispered.

The prince rushed over to Sleeping Beauty. His heart leapt as he gave her a gentle kiss.

"You must be my true love," smiled the princess, opening her eyes.

At that very moment, everybody in the castle woke up. It was as if no time had passed at all.

The prince and princess were married the very next day. The kingdom rang with bells and dancing filled the streets. All of the good fairies came to join in the celebrations.

The bad fairy was furious when she heard that her curse was broken. She disappeared, leaving the prince and Sleeping Beauty to live happily ever after.

GOLDILOCKS AND THE THREE BEARS

T HERE WERE ONCE three bears – a big Daddy Bear,
a middle-sized Mummy Bear and a little Baby Bear.
The bears lived together in a cottage in the woods.
    Every morning, Mummy Bear made porridge for breakfast.

One day, after Mummy Bear had cooked the
porridge, she poured it into three bowls.

"It's too hot to eat now," she said. "Let's go for
a stroll while it cools down."

Daddy Bear shut the door and off they went. Nobody
noticed the little girl hiding in the garden.

The little girl was called Goldilocks. Feeling curious, she lifted the latch on the door and crept inside to look around.

The bears' cottage was warm and cosy. The kitchen dresser was stacked with cheery plates and happy pictures lined the walls.

"Breakfast!" gasped Goldilocks, spying the kitchen table. It had been set for three. There was a big bowl, a middle-sized bowl and a tiny bowl. Each one was full of creamy porridge.

Goldilocks took a mouthful of porridge from the big bowl on the table.

"Oh no!" she cried. "It's much too hot!"

Goldilocks looked over at the middle-sized porridge bowl.

"I'll just try a mouthful," she whispered, hungrily lifting the spoon to her lips.

"Ugh!" spluttered Goldilocks. "It's much too lumpy!"

There was only one bowl left to try. The girl moved round to the little green bowl with bees painted round the edge.

"I'll try a little bit," she decided.

The porridge in the little bowl smelled especially delicious. Goldilocks pulled up a chair and dipped in the spoon lying alongside it.

"Mmmm…!" she beamed. "This porridge is just right."

This breakfast wasn't too hot and it wasn't too lumpy. The little girl liked it so much she ate it all up.

Goldilocks couldn't resist tiptoeing into the bears' cosy living room. Three chairs stood in front of her, arranged in a neat row.

Goldilocks climbed on to the tall chair. "Oh no," she frowned. "This is much too hard!"

The girl walked over to the pink middle-sized chair.
She sank deep into the cushions.

"Definitely not!" said Goldilocks. "This one is much
too soft!"

There was only one chair left to try.

"This chair is just right," she smiled, before the leg broke
with a loud snap!

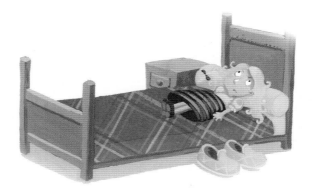

All this made Goldilocks feel tired. She crept into the
bears' bedroom.

"This bed is much too hard," sighed the girl, lying on the
big blue bed.

She jumped on to the middle-sized bed next, but it was
much too soft.

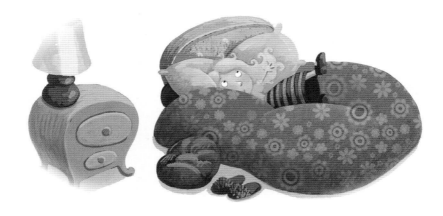

Finally, Goldilocks rested her head on the littlest bed.
"This bed is just right," she murmured, drifting off to sleep.

Just then, the three bears returned from their walk. Daddy Bear looked round the kitchen.

"Who's been eating my porridge?" he bellowed in a booming voice.

Mummy Bear stared at the splodges on the tablecloth.

"Who's been eating my porridge?" she cried.

Baby Bear ran up to the table and peered into his bowl. His breakfast had disappeared.

"Who's been eating my porridge?" he gasped. "It's all gone!"

Mummy Bear comforted Baby Bear while Daddy Bear strode into the living room.

"Who's been sitting in my chair?" growled Daddy Bear, getting even more cross.

Mummy Bear spotted her cushions and knitting spread all over the floor.

"Who's been sitting in my chair?" she cried.

Mummy and Daddy Bear turned round to look at Baby Bear.

Baby Bear pointed at his little green seat.

"Who's been sitting in my chair?" he sobbed.
"It's been broken in two!"

Mummy and Daddy Bear marched into the bedroom.

"Who's been sleeping in my bed?" frowned Daddy Bear.

The blankets had been disturbed and a slipper knocked on to the floor.

Mummy Bear took one look at the rumpled blanket before her.

"Who's been sleeping in my bed?" she cried.

Suddenly, Baby Bear tugged at his mother's sleeve.

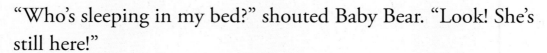

"Who's sleeping in my bed?" shouted Baby Bear. "Look! She's still here!"

Goldilocks woke up with a start.

"Oh my!" she squealed, running out of the bedroom and down the stairs.

Goldilocks fled out of the door and into the woods. She didn't stop until the cottage was far behind her. The three bears never saw the naughty girl again.

THE UGLY DUCKLING

ONE FINE DAY a mother duck sat on her nest, waiting for her eggs to hatch.

"When will my babies come?" she wondered. "It can't be long now!"

Sure enough, she soon heard a little pecking sound.
Each of her eggs began to crack open.

Six of the ducklings were fluffy and sweet. The
duck was delighted.

But one of the ducklings was much larger than the rest. He was gangly and grey. Even his mother thought he was ugly.

The mother duck led her brood to the water's edge. The six yellow ducklings waddled into the pond, splashing and cheeping all the while.

"Those six are such sweet ducklings," said the other ducks and geese. "But who is that ugly creature at the back?"

The awkward grey duckling swam in lonely circles round the pond. No one wanted to play with him and nobody wanted to talk to him. Even his own brothers and sisters turned up their little beaks when he swam by.

Word quickly spread. Soon the poor creature was known only as the Ugly Duckling.

The Ugly Duckling grew a little bigger, but he still looked different from the rest of his family.

"You must leave the pond," said his mother. "You don't fit in here."

The other ducklings snuggled together as he sadly swam away.

The Ugly Duckling walked forlornly
through a farm. He had nowhere to go.

A cow wandered across the meadow to
take a look at the strange-looking bird.

"Hello," quacked the Ugly Duckling.
"Can I be your friend?"

The cow looked surprised.
　　"You are an ugly thing," she replied.
"You don't fit in here."

The poor Ugly Duckling felt his heart sink. He waddled on until he came to the farmhouse. A large tabby cat leapt down to meet him.

"Hello," quacked the Ugly Duckling. "Can I be your friend?"

The cat chased the duckling out of the yard.

"You are an ugly thing," she hissed. "You don't fit in here."

Time passed and autumn set in. The Ugly Duckling was bigger now, but he still had the same dowdy feathers and clumsy webbed feet.

One day he met a rabbit hopping through the forest.

"Hello," quacked the Ugly Duckling. "Can I be your friend?"

The rabbit stared at the strange grey bird.

"You are an ugly thing," he sniffed. "You don't fit in here."

The days grew shorter and the nights grew colder. The Ugly Duckling waddled all over the land, but nobody wanted to talk to him. He felt happiest curled up alone, hiding himself from the world.

One day a boy discovered the Ugly Duckling trembling behind a fallen tree.

"Hello," quacked the Ugly Duckling. "Can I be your friend?"

The boy wrinkled his nose in horror.

"You are an ugly thing," he scowled. "You don't fit in here."

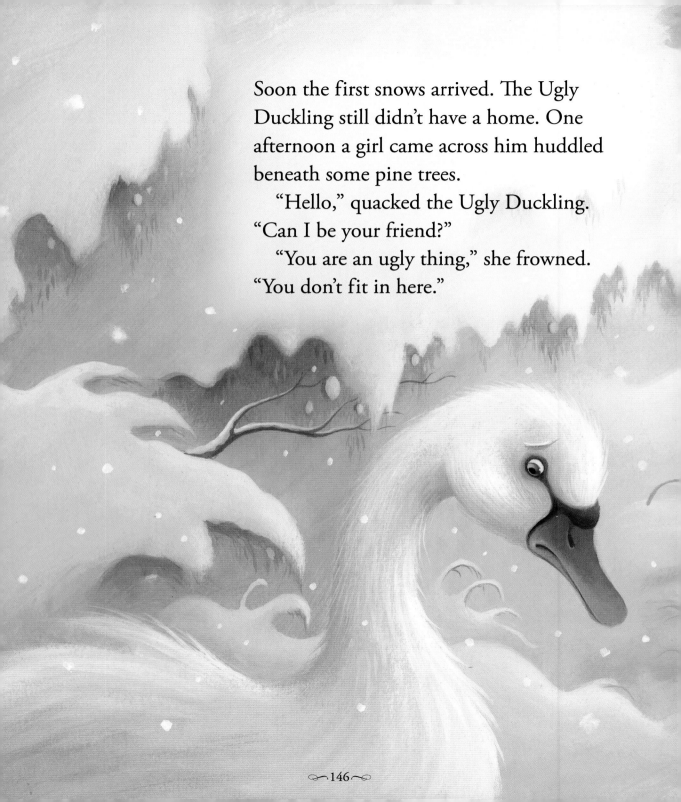

Soon the first snows arrived. The Ugly
Duckling still didn't have a home. One
afternoon a girl came across him huddled
beneath some pine trees.

"Hello," quacked the Ugly Duckling.
"Can I be your friend?"

"You are an ugly thing," she frowned.
"You don't fit in here."

Soon it was winter. With a heavy heart the Ugly Duckling returned to his pond. The frozen waters were cold and lonely, but at least there was nobody there to tease him.

"One day I will fit in," sighed the duckling, looking up to the snowy skies.

The Ugly Duckling made a little bed in the reeds. Here the months passed slowly but peacefully. The humble creature didn't notice his feathers turning milky white. He didn't see how fine and strong his wings had grown.

One day the sun began to melt away the ice and snow. Spring had arrived at last!

Three stunning swans glided across the pond. The duckling curved his neck to hide his ugliness.

"Take a look in the water, friend," cried the swans.

The Ugly Duckling was astonished by his own reflection – he had grown into a beautiful white swan!

He spread his wings with joy. Soon he was soaring high into the air, gliding into the sunrise with the other swans. He would never be lonely again.